Tobacco Wars

Tobacco Wars

Paul Seesequasis

QUATTRO BOOKS

Copyright © Paul Seesequasis 2010

The use of any part of this publication, reproduced, transmitted in any form or by any means, electronic, mechanical, photocopying, or otherwise stored in an electronic retrieval system without the prior consent (as applicable) of the individual author or the designer, is an infringement of the copyright law.

The publication of *Tobacco Wars* has been generously supported by the Canada Council for the Arts and the Ontario Arts Council.

 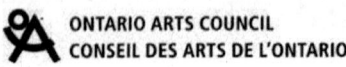

Cover art: Mary Anne Barkhouse
Cover design: Diane Mascherin
Typography: Grey Wolf Typography

Library and Archives Canada Cataloguing in Publication

Seesequasis, Paul
  Tobacco wars / Paul Seesequasis.

ISBN 978-1-926802-12-1

  1. Jonson, Ben, 1573?-1637--Fiction. 2. Pocahontas, d. 1617--Fiction.
I. Title.

PS8637.E4455T62 2010   C813'.6   C2010-905324-9

Novella Series #15
Published by Quattro Books Inc.
89 Pinewood Avenue
Toronto, Ontario, M6C 2V2
www.quattrobooks.ca

Printed in Canada

Adeena, this one is yours

In the beginning there was only a Bear.

Bear Woman spits, her phlegm-addled missile sends an uproarious orange iridescent flame ball high into the night sky. She scratches her thick, hairy thighs with her pointed claws, sending fleas and ticks scurrying, topsy-turvy, for cover, and with a deep breath, she raises one cheek from the log and lets loose a bellowing fart, that resounds through the darkened Cornwall woods, sending great horned-ears flapping toward the stars with a chorus of echoing hoots.

Bear Woman yawns, her gaping jaw and yellow fangs glinting off the fire, then pokes the flames with her cane. And waits for the boy. The boy whom nightly she pulls down between her thighs, so that he can lap at the honey hive of creation, her juices of inspiration, her slit of inspiring superstitions. She has raised him since she rescued the boy, years ago, from the St. Michael's residential school. He had been a mere waif then, no more than six summers aged, but his angelic face had smitten her as she had hunched over him that night, her breath blowing back his black hair.

This, after she had killed the nun who walked the hallways, with one swipe of her mighty paw, sending the head rolling down the hallway and out the door – a death too sudden and painless, she figured.

Bear Woman often stalked the halls of residential schools, late at night. Children were tidbits, yummy treats, but this time it was different. Here was a boy with potential, her very own water-boy, her servant, and her toy.

So she had abducted him that night, grabbing the waif with one swoop of her mighty arm, and then, rolling him into a fetal ball, had shoved him deep into her enormous anus, her sphincter closing on him, sheltering him like an impenetrable cocoon, as she bounded from the school on all fours, this time with no caution as alarms rang and startled pedophiliac custodians stumbled in their night clothes into the hallway, far too late to impede her escape.

Later, she shat him out, licked him clean with her two-foot tongue, and fed him, for the first time, from the life-giving fountain of her voluptuous vulva.

Thus was cemented a bond that would shake the new world, transcend artificial borders, revive timeless free trade routes, and, most of all, plant the seeds of that most illustrious crop: tobacco.

- altered history

Raw & gritty

Tobacco that outlandish weede
It spendes the braine and spoiles the seede
It dulls the spirite, it dims the sight
It robs the woman of her right.

– Dr. William Vaughn, 1617

Shores

It is late spring and she stands on the shoreline as a sail emerges. A small speck.

Nothing more.

At first Pocahontas thinks it is another gull, riding the sea breeze, but her heart betrays her as it beats faster. It is no bird. Across the green horizon the white speck takes shape, wings become sails. A hull emerges, slowly, ever so slowly. Her brothers, who have been silent till now, begin talking excitedly then run back to the camp.

She remains on the bluff.

Alone.

Watching.

The sea is unusually calm.

The sails become distinct, triple masts, furled, tacking the hard winds.

The sun rises in its arc 'cross the sky as the hull comes into full view, much scurrying on-board, and a single boat is lowered from the side.

"And so it begins," she says to herself.

Bear Woman squatted, thighs spread, buttocks scraping the tops of the jack pines, and pissed. A gushing, yellow torrent from her urethra. She pissed and pissed and pissed. The torrent formed a stream then a river, gurgling and gushing down the valley, sweeping away trees and rocks, sending animals scurrying and swimming for high ground.

The piss flowed down the valley, searching and finding the path of least resistance, through valleys, over ledges, pursuing a direction east, toward the rising sun, toward the first ocean. Bear Woman roared with satisfaction, her bladder nearly empty, as she surveyed what she had done. She grunted and peed some more till she was quite empty.

The river was a mighty channel, flowing where once had been dry land.

She then squatted again, over the torrent, thighs spread, and shat, turd after turd, each turd floating down the river of urine, until, catching on submerged tree branches, they anchored, forming a thousand islands.

Again, Bear Woman stood on her haunches, raised her snout, and smelled the pungent aroma of her feces and grinned.

Yes, it was as it was meant to be.

Islands of refuge.

Rivers of trade.

Arterial arteries that would outlast the coming floods.

Seeds

He has lost his wife and his infant child to the fevers, their remains left on a distant island. But he has his seeds. Those seeds that would bring an instant sentence of death were he to fall into the long reach of Papists. His precious seeds that have followed him: from the West Indies to the Americas, through storms, chases, shipwreck, and plague – to the Bermudas and now, finally, Jamestown.

The guilt over the loss of his wife and child lingers and John Rolfe ponders if it be the mighty hand of G-d punishing him for the fact that G-d knows that the loss of that bag of seeds, lovingly wrapped in leather and twine, would slice a wound far deeper in his soul than the recent loss of his dearly-departed. But he is grateful. He has finally landed on the American shores. He has arrived at his destination.

Jamestown is even less than he expected if that were possible. A ramshackle collection of wooden buildings, poorly kept, barren fields bearing failed crops and proficient weeds, and leaning fort walls, which would barely keep grazing deer out, let alone murderous savages. And a distressed and shambling parade of farmers, fortune seekers and traders, sickly and dispirited, who, it is soon evident, are completely reliant on the local Indians for food, medicine, and protection from other tribes.

"A more disadvantageous climate for an investment as potentially great and earth-shaking as my enterprise I have never encountered," he confesses one night to his male confidants in the Company of Fellow Virginians, after imbibing one warm ale too many. But he knows the spring is coming, the ground is thawing, and the time to plant his dream is nearing. He imagines tall crops, stalks of a new strain of tobacco, one that is resilient and fast-growing. John Rolfe has decided already he will dub the crop Orinoco, in honour of his hero, Sir Walter Raleigh, and in tribute to that magical river that leads, somehow, down some yet uncharted tributary, to the fabled City of Gold, El Dorado.

His preparations are nearly complete. He has exhausted his savings and spent his last shillings hiring hands to clear the forest and mind the crops for the summer. Thirty miles upstream on the James River his land awaits him. He has given all the metal tools and trinkets he can spare to the Indians to secure their blessing and protection from marauding hostiles for his planned plantation, and all is in place for this spring.

His tobacco, he knows in his heart of hearts, will, in the next few years, fuel the tongues of gentlemen in the public houses and clubs of London. It will cure unctuous moistures in young men, suppress the spread of syphilis in the streets, and become a currency more accepted and desired than the King's note itself. Yes, fortune will offer her blessing as long as he avoids the extended hands of Rome and Madrid and the Papish sentence of immediate death to a foreigner such as he, caught with tobacco seeds in his possession.

But John Rolfe's mind is being steadily pulled, as if in a strong tide, toward yet another image. It is the daughter of the local Chief he has met several times since his coming, a certain alluring beauty who lingers in his dreams and thoughts. She has been at every feast, trade and negotiation with the savages and he has found it increasingly difficult to expunge her from his thoughts.

She is heathen to the core but seems at comfort with civilized ways, dressed in a manner now almost approximating a proper lady, and has mastered the civilized tongue in an alarmingly quick fashion.

This woman, this Pocahontas, he repeats her name again in his mind, is a most enticing spectre haunting him.

Paul Seesequasis

Are you coming out of your hibernation? Bear.

Are you spreading your thighs for me? Is your honey pot dripping from six months of dreams?

Is that truly a traditional labia piercing you have?

Do those embedded trading post beads make you come when you move in that way?

Roll in the snow for me. Bear.

Squat on your haunches. Show your mound.

Share the source of the new world.

Open up for me. Let me see inside.

The spring is coming and you are melting the snows.

Bear.

Crops

She watches him as he surveys his fields. The September sun is hot, sticky and warm, insects buzz in the air, and the broad green leaves of Orinoco tobacco are ripe for picking. The workers have begun at one end of the field; whites, Negroes, Indians, alongside each other, some singing in their task, backs bent low, picking row after row of leaves. Endless wicker baskets are filled and passed back to a mule-drawn wagon where they are laid out for the countless barge-rides back to Jamestown. John Rolfe sits astride his white horse, pipe in mouth and broad-brimmed hat on head shading his fair pale skin from the ravages of the sun, and lords over his creation.

He is a peculiar man, Pocahontas decides, but not unappealing. Where there were once trees and bush, there is now a broad expanse of his plants, a full four feet high, radiant and softly swaying in the breeze. In a short season this man has changed the earth. And it is not his physical appearance that attracts her, for he is rather portly and slightly hunched, but his unshakable devotion to a dream, such an ingrained sense of mission, which she finds alluring. His first words to her were of tobacco and, since those first awkward utterances, that is all he has spoken to her of. He has expanded every effort to find time alone with her since then, and all summer he has told her of his plants, the cultivation of them, the process of drying them, packing them, and finally, the eventual epic voyage across the big waters to the great city of London.

He tells her they will "inspire the men's talk that leads to new ideas and greatness."

"I am following in Raleigh's footsteps," he explained to her a summer night a month ago, when she realized he was truly courting her. "Raleigh is a great man but his dream remains unfinished as he now languishes in prison in London with little hope of release. I shall fulfill the dream."

He had said this almost as a proposal as he took her hand in his for the first time.

"I shall realize Raleigh's vision and more than inspire commerce, which, in itself, is a worthwhile endeavour; my tobacco will inspire a greater world. It will push back the curtains of somnolence, fuel men's minds, and quicken the age of exploration. And all I desire, to achieve fulfillment, is you at my side."

Pocahontas has doubts he is any younger than her father, Wahunsenacawh, but this does not trouble her nor does the fact that there is little about him that stirs her heart or intrigues her in an intimate manner. That her father will approve, she has little doubt. His interests, she knows, are guided by what Wahunsenacawh feels is best for his people and, at heart, in the world of today's diplomacy, she knows she is more than a daughter now; she is a bargaining chip.

And, as John Rolfe is more than merely a man, but her ticket to a new world across the seas, she decides she will willingly partake in the game.

The specks of blood are black pools on white snow. Every few hundred feet they fall like errant raindrops from her vagina, silently marking her trail in the moonlight.

These small splashes betray her. She knows this. But the flow cannot be ebbed. She runs some more, as fast as her legs can carry her, through dark spruce and towering jack pine, her breath clouding the frigid air. She pauses, catching her breath, her breasts rising and falling as her lungs painfully try to take in the cold air. A million stars look down upon her but no angels descend from the heavens. There is no salvation.

Near her a tree cracks in the cold and she jumps in fear. Eyes widen but there is nothing but a lingering moan as the trunk splits. The young woman exhales and crouches. She listens and for a moment hope delicately springs forth. Then she hears them in the distance. The muffled barking as they direct each other, losing then recovering her scent trail, discovering each little blood spot, then barking excitedly as each frozen droplet becomes fresher.

— She runs again. —

Putting raised forepaw forward he pauses.

She is close now, he can not only smell but sense her. He feels a stirring in his scrotum. His hidden sheath stirs. A younger male scampers past him excitedly, almost bounding, and the older wolf bares his fangs and snarls a warning, and the younger wolf backs off, tail down. The four younger males circle expectantly as the elder raises his muzzle and sniffs the air.

He smells her.

His ears peel back and he howls before bounding forward, tail raised. — He sights her. — There is no escape, no point. She stops and turns as they approach. Watching, amber and gold eyes gaze at her. But only one tail is raised and it is the elder male.

He sits on his haunches, farther back as the younger ones circle her. Watching.

Thick tongues emerge from muzzles, seeming to grin at her. But the younger males keep their distance as she looks to the older wolf, meets his stare, and nods. He rises and moves toward her. – She turns. – She falls forward on all fours, ass raised as the wolf mounts her.

On his hind legs, forelegs on her shoulders, he enters her as the bone from his sheath extends; narrow it penetrates her now puffy labia. She feels it enter but barely. She buries her head in her arm as he pumps, moving from leg to leg as his flaccid penis slowly engorges inside her and the blood flows. So unlike a human, she thinks, erect after penetration but not before.

His knot expands, binding them together. In response her vaginal muscles tighten. She pulls forward.

He thrusts rapidly, panting, and then spurting into her as they both collapse. Still bonded, they lie still on the snow, as the young males circle, watching but silent.

Only the lead wolf howls at the moment of creation.

Stimulus

"Gaze your eyes upon this, my dear. This be the stimulus that shall quicken our pace, put fortitude in our endeavours, ensure our supremacy over the scheming Papists in damned Rome, bankrupt the corrupt King of Spain, and guarantee the success of our global enterprise," John Rolfe says, rubbing his hands together.

Pocahontas says nothing but watches as sack after sack of tobacco is carried up the plank on toiling backbones of sweating workers in the October sun and then passed down into the hold of the over-laden vessel.

She ponders this now, on the dock of Jamestown, which is now abuzz with activity. How much everything has changed in the short season since her husband has landed on these shores. She wonders, secretly, whether she is an ambassador for her people still, or now a betrayer, complicit in the Englanders' evident independence and growing confidence. A few years ago she felt pity for these sickly, child-like settlers and had gladly urged her father to adopt them as one would adopt the children of enemy tribes beaten in battle. But now she feels a certain trepidation, a cloud of dark foreboding, and it seems to her that her husband has become the spark to the dangerous powder keg, which is about to alight and explode her world apart.

"Our endeavours?" she asks.

He looks at her, taken aback.

"Of course, my dear. Our endeavours indeed, for they shall, as well, lift your people assuredly from darkness, from a dependency upon the vagaries of the natural world, and give you entry into the light of civilization. We are allied in this, you and I, and your people shall benefit immensely from Our Majesty's benevolence. He is a Monarch of His word and treaties sacred and true will guarantee all He says."

She sighs.

"I see that we were no worse off before your arrival. Perhaps a trinket or two less that we did not have, but one does not want what one cannot imagine. Nor was the odd musket or shovel needed, and would I trade in hindsight all the joy of my childhood, or playing with my brothers, for this? Perils and dangers beyond our lands we did face, and yes we could manage them, but now, I fear, there is a threat far greater than any of our Elders could prophesize," she concludes.

"How so?"

"It is as if a new day has dawned and all that is familiar has become strange. We find illness now that did not exist a few years prior, and we become attached, smitten, seduced, by all this in Jamestown and, with respect," she bows slightly, "it perhaps lessens us, a little more each day."

"You worry too much, my dear." John Rolfe pats her arm gently, and then reaches for his pipe. "What corruptions there are will pass. Trust me. The mark of progress is a blessing true and the concept is merely new to you. G-d in His wisdom has brought us here. Have faith in His intentions, for the riches will come, assuredly, to us both."

Pocahontas nods, for a moment tempering her fears.

She closes her eyes and tries to picture London. But despite all the stories and descriptions she has heard from the Jamestown owners, she is unable to conjure an image that satisfies her.

It will be strange, elusive, beyond every notion she possesses, is what she decides.

It was Wolverine, that wily entrepreneur, who is generally credited with establishing the first smokeshop. It was another time, old times, and Bear Woman's turds had recently hardened, fertilizing grasses, trees, flowers and wondrous new herbs. Wolverine was an inquisitive sort, given to experimentation, a compulsive masturbator, and always on the lookout for some new high.

He had consumed countless varieties of hallucinogenic mushrooms, white ones, red, spotted, orange, black, and he had chewed every fungus he found on old tree trunks, nurtured by the Holy Shit of Bear Woman. But each high, no matter how euphoric, only left Wolverine with a constant craving for something new.

"You are nothing but a dreamer," Bear Woman had scoffed, to which Wolverine could only snicker in agreement.

"But perhaps over there you will find something new for your jaded palate." Bear Woman gestured, pointing to a rise in the distance, to which Wolverine glanced, squinting, and saw familiar leafy plants growing.

"Bah, more smoke weed. Old lady, what do I want more of that for?" Wolverine sneered, to which Bear Woman responded with a resounding swipe of her paw, sending Wolverine rolling down the hill, blood splattering on the grass.

"Insolent fool. Not the cannabis. Beyond that, those large-stemmed plants. Yeah, those. Go. Go. Try one." Bear Woman pointed a silver claw.

Nodding, Wolverine, more fearful than curious, stumbled over to the broader-leafed plants, picked a leaf and, glancing over to Bear Woman for approval, popped it in his mouth and chewed.

The taste was not unpleasant, strong, pungent, and as he chewed, the pleasure grew.

There were no illuminating visions, no miraculous dreams, no body rush, no instant erection, but there was a sweet, gentle buzz, like bees dipping into honey, and Wolverine was smitten.

Days passed and Wolverine chewed and chewed, spitting out the little tobacco balls until they coalesced into greater and greater balls, finally becoming what would, in modern times, be known as the Gatineau Hills. Then Bear Woman motioned him over, and Wolverine crawled to her. She squatted, reached behind her and with one hairy paw spread a buttock, and farted, sending Wolverine scurrying behind a tree.

"You are creating something?" Wolverine asked, fully knowledgeable of the wonders of her anus. Bear Woman chuckled, nodded her massive head, then reached into her Holy Orifice and pulled out a wooden box.

Wolverine was perplexed.

Bear Woman handed him the box.

"Matches," she replied with a grin, yellow fangs flashing. "You light them on the side of the box."

Wolverine lit and there was a spark, a carbon flash, and then flame. He giggled.

"With these I could burn the whole forest down," he chuckled, gesturing around him.

"No you won't," Bear Woman said. "With these you will light those broad green leaves upon which you have been gorging yourself. First,

you shall dry them, then pound them on a rock, wrap them in dry birch bark, put one end in your mouth, light the other, and inhale." And thus, Bear Woman created the first cigarette, or at least gave the idea to Wolverine, for Wolverine would, being a Wolverine, claim credit anyway.

Within a year Wolverine smokeshops spread across the land. Wolverine took out a patent, established franchises along ancient arterial trade routes, and reveled in the trade of tobacco.

Corruption

The herb-scented cloth Pocahontas holds to her face does little to mask the plague's stench. She has been warned away by the ship's surgeon, told there is no hope for her husband, and that she too will surely succumb to its grip should she choose to be near him; all this she has ignored. Let death take her, she will not forsake John Rolfe in his final, miserable moments.

The red sores have spread from his arms and legs to his whole body. Pus and blood fester and flow freely as his skin seems to crack and open of its own will, letting the soul drain out. His color has gone from pink to dark purple and when he tries to open his mouth to speak, it is bile and vomit that spews forth. In the darkest, farthest hold of the ship he lies in his hammock in which he was carried by worried sailors who crossed themselves and hurriedly deposited him to this secluded place. They will only return, when the time comes, to quickly sew the hammock shut and then bring it, one last time, to the deck, where John Rolfe will be consigned forever to the depths of the cold sea.

Only a single beeswax candle provides light and Pocahontas faithfully lights it each time the flame sputters and dies. The creaking of the timbers of the ship's hull against the ceaseless pressures of the cold Atlantic is, other than his labours, and her soft breathing, the only sound.

She applies a cold rag to suppress his fever. She does not know if it provides any comfort in his final moments, but it dispels slightly her feeling of overwhelming futility. She almost desires the fever to take her too, but for whatever reason it refuses the embrace.

Not knowing anymore what she can do, she softly sings a mourning song she had learned as a child.

She is softly singing in her language when he opens his eyes and for the first time in days she sees his soul. He looks at her and there is not fear but peace within.

Then he is gone.

She does not call for the sailors immediately but pulls out a thread and needle of her own and gently sews the hammock together.

Only after it is sewn tight does she climb up from the hold and, for the first time in three days, allow the sun's light to bathe her.

It is bright in the sky and at the high point of its journey. Pocahontas feels its warmth.

Tobacco Wars

And so it was that in May 1613, Samuel de Champlain came upon a Wolverine smokeshop on a small island near what is now Ottawa. As the Frenchman had no pelts to trade and was low on shiny baubles, he was forced to barter, finally parting with a perfectly good astrolabe, in order to secure a carton of cigarettes.

Champlain, who was not much given to bodily pleasures, found an exception with these strange, tube-like sticks. So impressed was he, that upon returning to France that winter, he presented his last pack of smokes to His Most Royal Majesty, King Louis XIII.

Soon, Royal Charters were granted, ships and fleets assembled, and cartons upon cartons of cigarettes were making their way across the great waters. Though rich by now, Wolverine was troubled. He had constantly searched for innovations to improve his product. Birchbark was fine, but Wolverine found the skins of Jesuit missionaries to afford a much more satisfying smoke. Jesuit missionaries were plentiful, he reasoned, and would hardly be missed, so in 1649 the first productions began.

With a sharp knife and a good fire, the first new cigarettes were created. The fire itself was not a necessity to extract the skin, but it did make for nice entertainment for all, and thus began a new sport that would soon become a tradition in itself and become known as Priest burning.

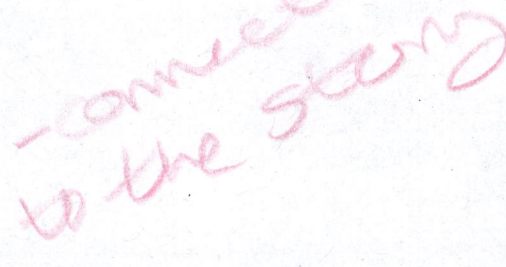

London

Shit. Everywhere shit and mud. The rain pours down, soaking the narrow streets and cobbled alleys as the carriage slowly, painfully, makes it way through huddled masses. Faces peer into her carriage window. A toothless man with one eye missing, his socket black and pussed, reaches in a three-fingered hand, begging for coins, before her chaperone slaps it away. A moment later, a young urchin runs up, sticking in her arms, in one hand what appears to be a hardened loaf of bread and in the other an outstretched empty palm, before she too is unceremoniously swatted away.

Still more rain, falling so fast and thick Pocahontas can barely see. They turn an alleyway and halt as a gang of drunken young men surges by, pushing and ripping through the crowd without pause. She sees a sword drawn, and a moment later a portly man falls to his knees, run through. Vendors shout from curbsides, fruits, breads, ales, fortunes, broadsheets of the daily news, children selling themselves, skinny dogs, a basket of hens; and a rat hunter with a long pole slung over his shoulder, twenty dead rodents hanging from their tails, winks at her as the carriage passes.

Then, quickly as it began, the rain stops.

As if through an invisible curtain, the hackney carriage passes near St. James Palace and the crowds dissipate. She sees more soldiers and then less pushing and more strolling as the refinement of clothing becomes apparent.

"We are entering better London," her chaperone informs her and, as the carriage rounds a corner, she sees broad skirts, felt hats, umbrellas and well-fed dogs on leashes. On a broad expanse, several clutches of men are standing, frilled and laced, yards apart, hitting what appear to be coloured balls with t-shaped sticks.

"Paille Maille," the chaperone explains, and she nods.

It seems so much tamer, so much slower, so, well, boring a sport in comparison to what she knows at home, and at that she smiles.

"And there," her chaperone points, almost touching her bosom with the sweep of his arm across her chest, "is your welcoming party. The Royal playwright Ben Jonson and his assorted admirers."

Pocahontas looks to see a tall, rather skinny, red haired man in a purple jacket, yellow felt hat and maroon breeches, sword on his hip, surrounded by a party of men and women in their patterned brocades, linen chemise and embroidered coifs, waiting for her, a smile on his lips.

Gathering her skirt above her ankles, she takes a deep breath as the carriage comes to a halt and her door is opened.

She steps out as the playwright extends his hand.

A certain Jesuit, Jean de Brébeuf, inspired a new brand, Brébeuf's Best, made from the Jesuit's own delicately smoked skin, and the brand was so popular that Wolverine sold them in limited edition boxed sets.

But as time went on, and time was going on quicker now, as clocks were brought to Bear Woman's land by the newcomers, Wolverine found himself under increased pressure. The papers of various Kings and Queens were granting titles to new franchises, controlled by the newcomers, and increasingly Wolverine smokeshops were pushed aside.

In a panic, Wolverine sought audiences with various monarchs but was rejected. He turned to traditional copyright and sovereign entitlement but was overturned in court. Finally, he turned around, held his massive penis in his hands, and pissed in the general direction of Europe, before skulking off into the woods, never to be seen again.

Masque

Pocahontas leans forward in the Royal Dais to better see the masked dancers below her on the stage. The extravagant colours of the costumed masked performers enthrall her, and the songs they sing, while strangely unmusical to her ear, are not unpleasant. It is a masque; this she knows, as it has been explained to her a dozen times already. Of course it is; they *are* wearing masks, she giggles to herself. How well she has done too with the etiquette upon meeting the King of England, who now sits not an arm's stretch from her. She has met the composer, a certain Ben Jonson, who, upon setting eyes on her, has done little else but stare, and later whispers in her ear that she must dance "au naturel like a sauvage pour moi." She also notices his trying to peer down her tight bodice as he presses forward as if to embrace, and she pulls back with a disapproving turn of her head.

But whatever dark carnal thoughts possess him, his masque is quite enchanting, and enthralls enough to let her momentarily forget the compression of her breasts within the binding corset. Such flamboyantly costumed characters, such pastoral and idyllic staging, and the actors' names as they introduce themselves to the audience – Delight, Harmony, Grace, Love, Laughter, Revel, Sport and Wonder – are equally seductive. Each introduction is followed by an extravagant bow and lowering of mask. The King himself, the scent of his perfumed hair dizzying her, leans over and whispers in her ear that the play is a celebration of the coming of spring; and for a moment Pocahontas saddens, wonders if she will be back to see the snows melt and the new buds rising in the forest she knows.

But for now she sits mesmerized, not aware that half the eyes in the theatre are trained, not on the stage, but on her, the savage princess from the Americas whose beauty, brown skin, and perfect white teeth have set the courts atwitter and have high society tingling with girlish chatter. In her blue embroidered jacket, emblazoned with sequins and with black ribbons, her reticella of white starch rising around her slender neck, deep lace cuffs delicately falling over her wrists, and the soft, translucent yellow petticoat that frames her body, so daring in the Parisian manner, and that gives no evidence of any linen drawers underneath it all. She has ignited a mighty chorus of titters and envious glances from the young ladies of the Court and instigated a scrum of every fop and courtesan hoping to investigate if she truly is au natural under that teasingly lucent gown.

For Pocahontas, who back home has frolicked every summer naked with other children until the age of ten, the fuss and scandal over her body is at first deliciously new, but now she has already grown blasé with society's gaze. No, it is the masque that beguiles her, that ignites a spark for the theatrical, for that magic which is brought to the stage.

And, reassessing her earlier rebuff, she has set her thoughts now on its playwright.

Bear Woman sighed and rolled over.

She was conserving her energies for what she knew would be a long, long winter.

Outside, a world turned upside down.

Stars clashed and the moon exploded into a thousand shards of white that fluttered down over the land.

Smuts

"'Tis time you meet some practitioners of London's finest pleasures," Jonson exclaims as they step from the carriage. There are four of them in the party, with Burke and Hickey, two of Jonson's trusted companions from the Man-Killing club – we admit no man who has not killed a man – and all three men are tipsy from quaffing German wine and singing an odd song as Pocahontas steps onto the muddy street.

The smells of urine, sweat, horse shit, rotting vegetables and meats, and perfumes collide in a heady mix that for the moment overwhelms her. She teeters, and Burke, who has been extraordinarily attentive since they were introduced, notices and holds her steady. He inquires if she is alright and she nods, holding the perfumed kerchief to her face as she adjusts and regains her balance. What astounding sights and sounds she has witnessed in this strange city in only a few days. After a moment she recovers her composure but the smells still shock and rattle her; reminding her she is a stranger in a strange land. "Come, my lady, and meet some bunters, midnight mothers…," Jonson begins, and then is overtaken by Burke and Hickey, who join him in a chorus. "Blowzabellas, smuts, doxies, bun butters, cracks…in short, our whores; and here you will find them in all ages, sexes, sizes and inclinations."

"Princess Polly! Come here!" Burke exclaims loudly, and a young girl steps forward from the crowd gathered by Moorgate. She is adorned in a blue petticoat and has red and pink ribbons tied to her hair. Her lips are obscenely painted red. She struts over, licks Burke on the cheek then turns, her eyes riveting on Pocahontas.

"Aye, what 'ave we 'ere?" she inquires, peering close at Pocahontas and running a finger along her cheek. "And 'ere are you from? So brown and exotic like…China? India? Romania?"

Jonson laughs. "She is from the Americas. And is considered royalty among her people, so kindly don't touch the lady with your filthy whore's hand," he laughs, as he swats the red-lipped girl's hand away.

She pouts, sticks out her tongue, and does an exaggerated curtsey; and in that gesture Pocahontas can see that she is no more than a girl, barely of bleeding age, and only her eyes seem mature and careworn. She twirls around as Hickey goes to spank her, then she lifts her petticoat, flashing her bare mound, as Hickey cheers, wraps an arm around her thin waist, and disappears into the crowd with her, parting with a wave.

"He always goes for the virgins," Jonson says to Pocahontas, who looks at him, somewhat perplexed. Whoredom, not merely the concept of selling sexual favors, but its commonality and social acceptance in London society, astounds her. But more astounding yet is that such an obvious girl of the trade could remain a virgin.

"Surely she can't be?" she offers. To which Jonson interrupts with a laugh.

"Oh, it is a simple enough surgical procedure to replant, if you will, a maiden's honour, and indeed, it is one of the more higher paid and noble practices for physicians in our fair city. A girl with her maidenhood intact, even if for the 30th time that month, fetches far more guineas than a girl without; for many a discerning gentleman wishes to be deceived that it is he who has picked the flower and broken the seal. Many houses of the trade maintain their own physician on site, and provided a girl is young, has her teeth, and her maidenhead restored, she is as valuable as rare spice and requires little imagination. And if a gentleman refuses to pay the proper value to break it in, well there is another hole, which also comes at a higher price. It's a win-win scenario for the house as you see."

"Do you wish to partake my dear?" Burke asks from the other side. "We could arrange a little sample for you. Either girl or boy."

She shakes her head no as the crowd mills and surges around her. A vendor, with a basket on her head, walks by, chanting "Oranges and fair lemons," and this is more to her taste.

She leaves the men standing and bartering and walks over, passes a shilling to the old woman, takes a lemon, breaks the skin with her nails, and squeezes the acidic juice into her mouth.

Bear Woman huddles under the snow-laden blanket. The wind funnels between the high-rise offices, howling around her ears. The light of the streetlamp bathes her in a soft yellow glow. She raises her paw, wipes mucus from her running snout, and peers around.

"Where is the boy?" she growls. "I miss his soft skin, his little penis. His giggle."

She clutches the bottle of branvin in her other paw and brings it to her mouth, letting the warm liquid pour from the lip of the bottle, down her snout, some finding its way into her mouth. She pisses, feeling the warmth run down her thighs, soaking her ragged dress, dripping through the subway grate she is sitting on.

"The boy is missing. Oooh. And where are the wolves? This was their territory. They marked it. Hunted deer, tore into flanks of succulent, dripping flesh. Where is the hunt now?"

She peers around, up and down the street, and harrumphs.

A cop car slows down. A face peers out from the passenger window and a beam of bright light illuminates her face. A door opens and a cop steps out.

"Hey you. You alright?"

The cop steps forward to look at her but then steps back, the smell overwhelming him.

"Jesus. She stinks."

The other cop steps out from the driver's seat and walks around the cruiser.

"Damn. Hey you. It's pretty cold out here. You want us to call street patrol to take you to a shelter?"

She looks up from under her blanket and both cops step back. Beady eyes peer at them, yellow fangs glint from her grin. Bear Woman raises a forearm and waves them away.

"The wolves will get you. They will. Listen. They are coming. You dare transgress on their territory. They will come, bouncing and howling and hunting you. You are both dead meat. Run. Run now and you may be spared. Run now and you may not feel them tear into your throats, your ribs, and your balls. They will tear you into pieces. Suck your marrow. They will…"

"Damn crazy Indian lady." The cop shakes his head, motions to his partner, and they get back into the cruiser and pull away.

Bread Street

Along Bread Street they stroll. It is a rare, rare, sunny afternoon and seemingly all of London is out and about on the streets and alleys.

"'Tis Friday and our destination is there," Jonson says, pointing to the tavern sign and an odd portrait of a full-bosomed woman who, from the waist down, it appears, is a fish. Pocahontas ponders this, but before she can inquire she is whisked inside, amongst the familiar smoke stench of tobacco and the aroma of old ale.

A tall, handsome man stands and bellows above the din, "Ben!" and the playwright takes her arm and leads her to the table at the back corner where the tall man bows, kisses her hand and smiles, rather mischievously.

"Inigo Jones, Madame. And I am truly honored to meet such a beauty of nature. I have heard so much already. I must say, Madame, you have all the court of London abuzz."

Pocahontas studies his face and nods to him. She is now accustomed to the liberal usage of flattery and no longer blushes, but there is a spark to this man's eye which she likes, and as she takes her chair she smiles as Jonson yells out for three more tankards of ale.

"Welcome to the Friday Street Arts Club," Inigo says, resting his long fingers on her hand. "It is a rather exclusive club of two, I am afraid, and we are seldom graced by a lady's company. At least the type of woman that one may refer to with a lady present."

"You mean prostitutes," she says.

He laughs. "Indeed. Smuts are here on occasion, I am afraid. So to be in the company of a lady so, well, chaste, is a rare pleasure indeed."

"I see."

"And it is here," Inigo explains, "that every week your friend and I debate the finer points of this land's arts and settle, or should I say unsettle, the questions that plague the fine practice of the theatre."

"Bah," Jonson interrupts. "It is simply where we meet weekly to rehash an endless impasse. This is the place where the superior mind, such as I, is continually confounded by the inability of those of aesthetic sentiment to see beyond the frivolity of frills and lace."

Inigo guffaws loudly when Pocahontas raises a quizzical eyebrow.

"You see, my lady, Mr. Jonson here is of the mind that it is content – I should say words alone – that are the true measure of great theatre, whereas I, though designer and architect I confess to be, am of the mind that there is a greater whole to be considered, and that what he calls 'frills and lace' is, in fact, an essential, no, the essential, essence of the act of artistic creation. In other words, one is not subservient to the other."

Jonson taps her shoulder to draw her attention, frowning visibly at the lingering touch of the architect's hand on her shoulder.
"We live in an age where form has overtaken substance. It is barely a few decades since my muse, the one who, I dare say, is

the only one who compares to me, has died," Jonson declares empathically.

"He is referring to Shakespeare," Inigo interrupts, with a smirk. "He is fond of making that comparison."

"Indeed I am." Jonson frowns. "And in the time since his death, the eyes of the audience have grown accustomed to all forms of visual trickeries, gaudy embellishments, and costumed buffoonery."

At this Inigo snorts loudly as Jonson points to him.

"And here, with us, is the worst perpetrator of this degeneration, this laziness, this sad age of distraction."

Inigo turns to her, ignoring the playwright.

"Madame, you were witness, I believe, to His Majesty's masque a fortnight ago."

Pocahontas nods, not liking where this is going.

"And pray tell, then," he casts an eye at Jonson, "what sticks most in your memory? The fine staging, lighting and costuming of the actors principal or the words they rehearsed by memory to impart? Rather, could you imagine simply those words and an absence of all finery?"

"Pah!" Jonson exclaims.

Pocahontas ignores the playwright. Rather she does more than ignore, she sits forward, her tight bosom accentuated by her new posture, and almost leans into Inigo.

"Well, it be true that I see a unity of the two," she offers. "Obviously it is not evident in this ale-fueled debate with its two composers so seemingly at odds. But the words were of true beauty, and while I cannot recite, or even indeed remember the bulk, it is of little matter, as I have full confidence they spoke to me in a moving manner."

Jonson laughs, and sips triumphantly from his ale.

"Still, when I look fondly back I see the colours of the costumes, the make-up of the actors, the elaborate finery of the stage, and I smile. Those are not words, but they are wed to them in a pairing that, in my opinion, is heaven-inspired in its perfection."

At this Inigo stands and bows, taking her hand and planting a quick kiss.

"With that I must confess to a certain urgency in the need to piddle and beg of you permission to take leave, my lady." Pocahontas giggles, aware of the frowning playwright beside her. On Inigo's departure to the back door of the inn, Jonson turns to her, a certain disapproving flash in his eyes.

"Are you simply always so flirtatious? Well, you most certainly made an impression on him."

She shrugs, not quite convincingly, and turns to Jonson.

"I assure you, Sir, it is entirely without intent."

Bear Woman sits. Hears the wind howl but no wolves. She sits on her haunches, farts, and then starts to ramble down the street. Her ears pick up a sound. Rhythmic. Heavy thudding. Not tribal but music nonetheless. She turns to the wind, raises her head and sniffs. Chanel. Pierre Cardin. Human sweat. She sets off at a rapid gait, in the direction of the music.

She turns the corner and her little eyes are lit up by flashing lights, illuminated billboards, neon words, and headlights. Sexy people on the street turn and move aside, smelling her before seeing her.

Bear Woman sees a queue of people and rambles toward it.

One of the doormen in his double-breasted Armani suit sees her first.

"What the fuck?" He nudges his colleague, who is preoccupied with letting only the prettiest of girls in, and he also turns to look.

"Shit, that's the biggest and ugliest bag lady I've ever fuckin' seen," he says to his partner, and they both watch incredulously as the shambling brown form draws ever closer. The pretty people pull back, young women cover their mouths, and their boyfriends stare wide-eyed, overwhelmed by this wild, stinking visage that has emerged from the darkness of the night.

Bear Woman shambles ahead as the two doormen now move forward, the larger man now waving his arms at her.

"Get lost, you crazy lady! This is a club, not a homeless shelter. Get the fuck outta here."

His partner steps beside him, arms crossed, staring at her. She peers up at them, on all fours now, her snout at crotch level. She can smell the cologne they have splashed over their thighs, under *their Zimmerli boxers, in anticipation of blowjobs later from e-bombed young girls.*

Bear Woman snarls.

The larger doorman chuckles, then goes to boot her hard with his steel-toed shoe. His leg is in mid-kick as her forepaw rises with lightning speed and her claws grasp his scrotum through his pants, and rip. He screams, falling to the ground as red blood flows from his crotch. The other doorman reaches for the pistol in his overcoat at the same moment her other paw tears across his face, sinking four deep grooves into his flesh while blood spurts down. He falls to his knees, screaming.

People pull back. Running. Crying. Scattering. Screams echo. Bear Woman stands on her haunches, upright, all seven feet of her, raises her head and bellows to the night sky as the sound of sirens draws near.

She plops down and bounds away on all fours into the snowy streets. Seeking the boy.

Missing the wolves.

Ice

Dark black coal smoke hangs low, clouding the London skyline, pushed down by the cold weight of arctic air, while the carriage forces its way through teeming lanes of bundled walkers. Pocahontas huddles under a thick blanket, Jonson at her side. Their driver curses loudly at the throngs in his guttural voice and cracks his whip as they force the cab down the edge of the bank of the Thames, and onto the thick ice of the frozen river.

Coaches ply up and down the Thames from Westminster to the Temple. Tents of all colours and sizes are lined in uneven rows and smoke rises from numerous fires shadowing more smoke into the black canopy overhead. Jonson and Pocahontas transfer to another sled.

"On skeetes to move faster," Ben Jonson explains; and then they are off, racing among the other skeeted carriages, circling a track while the throngs mingle and buzz and drink and cheer amidst the tented ice city.

She closes her eyes, feeling the cold air brush past her face, until they finally stop, and, taking the playwright's arm, she walks with him among the tented stalls, the puppet plays, the food sellers, the magicians, fortune tellers, broadsheet carriers and ale vendors. They buy some warmed cider, quaff it, and then Pocahontas has her palm read. The wrinkled reader, with her grey disheveled hair and beaded scarf, is at first taken with and distracted by Pocahontas' tattooed hand when she holds it.

"The future is bright and full of adventure," she explains, "until...," and she looks up at her with a certain hesitation, "until a sudden misfortune." Pocahontas does not ask more, just pulls her hands away and nods while an annoyed Ben Jonson hands over a coin: less than what is to be expected, but then the teller is not meant to tell such disquieting endings.

And then the roar of the nearby crowd draws them in. There is a circular enclosure and they push and squeeze their way to a vantage point where they can see a circular pit and within it a bear, chained to a large pole in the air and roaring and swatting and bleeding from numerous gashes in its thick brown hair. Around the beast, a dozen dogs swirl, pounce and snarl, lunging and running away. A few caught by the bear are claw-ripped and sent flying through the air. On the ice five or six dogs lie dead or dying. With each blow there is a gasp from the crowd, a cheer from some and moans from others.

"There is much wagering going on amongst the rabble," Ben Jonson yells in her ear, "petty pennies mostly, but for this poor crowd it is more than a rich man's fortune on the line. A poor man's sport to be sure."

She is oblivious to his words. She sees, in that moment, only the red eyes of the beast. Their eyes meet and she senses the bear's terror and its anger. The beast's awareness that its death is soon to come is clear. She pulls off her fur-lined mitt, the one the playwright had bought for her from the boutique of London's most prestigious leathermaker, and given to her with such expectation of gratitude, rolls it into a ball and, standing on her toes, tosses it with all her strength into the pit.

It lands but a short distance from the wounded bear's snout. The bear pauses, considers it, then, resting on its forelegs, lays its massive head down and sniffs it. The anger subsides as the beast's inner peace rises, and it ceases to fight, sits on its haunches, looks up toward the crowd, sees Pocahontas, and stares as the enraged dogs descend.

Running and snarling outside the Beaver Theatre the pack congregates. The bounty hunters are gone. The city walls have been breached. The urban domesticity has been torn asunder.

In The Beaver Theatre a lone generator powers the film projector whose image flickers and fades on the screen. She sits alone in the theatre, watching the obscure porno "She Does It with Wolves." The young woman smirks, watching, sound muted, as a "wolf" mounts the actress on the screen. The actress is on all fours, naked except for a feathered headband, head lowered, submissive.

She had found the silver canister buried underneath pile after pile of pornographic films. Labeled "Zoo," it had caught her eye, then the title and the peeling dried masking tape with the felt-pen written words "for special screenings only."

But the film itself is a downer. In and out of focus, sloppily edited, as if there were far too many takes, too many spoiled scenes; and finally, most disappointing are the "wolves." They are all domesticated dogs, shepherd-mixes, huskies, even a poodle; and she frowns.

There is no wildness. No biting, slavering passion in the animals. No boundless impetus. They seem almost reluctant, coaxed, cautious, as if they sense this is taboo.

She pats her protruding belly, feels the life inside.

Outside she hears the occasional howl and yelp from the circling pack. They are waiting for her.

But she lingers.

Lights a cigarette. Closes her eyes. And listens to the faint hum of the projector.

Penny University

Pocahontas finds it most curious that of the 40 or so men crammed into Jonathan's Coffeehouse, John Castaing, esteemed Huguenot broker, is the one seemingly most oblivious to the singular fact she is the only female presence in the smoky room. This is most remarkable to her, as she is sitting as close to him as is humanly possible and the tables and standing areas are crammed with philosophers, poets, actors, businessmen, soldiers, students and scoundrels, many of whom are eyeing her as if she were an exotic peacock, feathers ripe for the plucking.

But she has paid her penny to enter the 'university', and been escorted in by the King's playwright, and now she feels entitled to wrap her long fingers around this cup, sip this odd, dark, pungent brew, and listen to this strange but brilliant man.

John Castaing is enraptured by numbers on paper, which he places before her on the table while Ben Jonson rolls his eyes impatiently, wondering how this uniquely ugly man could be diverting the attention of his little princess away from him. What had been the perfect entrance, exotic woman on his arm, has turned suddenly, inexplicably, into a source of frustration. Ben Jonson slips a hand under the table and runs a finger along her smooth thighs, only to receive a sudden swat away, as if his hand were an unwelcome fly.

He sighs.

It's John Castaing's mind that intrigues her. Beyond the wart on his nose, the crooked and missing teeth, and the lisp, there is brilliance and, best of all, obsessive love in his every utterance on numbers. It is the genius of John Castaing that pulls her in.

At the moment, his fingers are excitedly pointing at numbers and calculations on paper, explaining the new course of exchange and how it – not muskets and cannons, not priests and Monarchs – will rule the world from this point forward.

"The true power is here," he says in his odd lisp. "Not in armies and churches or even gold and coins. The trick is knowing what people want, or think they want or must have, and when they can't get enough of it." He points to his coffee. "And that is the golden time; for surely, eventually, there will be too much, and it will saturate and rot, like a thin bag, and the bottom will drop."

John Castiang explains it is simply and ultimately numbers that lord over all.

"Written numbers, but each number carries the weight of the world. It's how you pick them, which ones you circle. But surely, it is more than chance or playing safe with it, for what has worked for today will stop working tomorrow. It is seeing the future and, more than that, making it happen. This," he says, pointing to the letters 8 and 23 and 47, "determines this. The risk is supreme and exhilarating."

His arms sweep the room.

"And over there," Pocahontas says, pointing to the west, toward her home, toward what they call the Americas, "these numbers will rule."

John Castiang looks to her in mild surprise. "Why do you say that?" He leans forward, listening intently.

"Because there," she turns to him and winks, pointing in the direction of her home, "what you call the 'Americas', is the future."

She holds his hand and squeezes.

"And this," her arms sweep the room, "will be eclipsed by that." She motions to the west.

"And your numbers will sweep across the great sea."

John Castiang claps in agreement.

Pocahontas smiles and turns.

"I shall live to see it."

Lapping at her labia, the boy learned ancient tongues. Bear Woman's folds parted, ever so slightly, allowing the whispers of a thousand new languages to seep out. Each fold, each crevice, emergent to another portal, to another higher language, and deeper, deeper whispers ever closer, closer to the source.

There was pleasure, of course, and at times Bear Woman moaned, her claws carved valleys in the earth, and her deep intake of breath brought the formless stars crashing down on her raised snout. She then exhaled, shooting the stars back into the black, black sky. Each time she came, she brought new stars down and shot them back, creating constellation after constellation, galaxy after galaxy.

Over time, the boy's tongue became adept, and soon the sky was a sprinkling, endless sea of stars; and while Bear Woman's enormous head created the universe, her mound whispered to the boy, a trillion words flowing through the sea of her juices, whole sentences arising on the swollen ridges, and the first songs from the depth of her slit. Each lick, every lap, at the fount of creation, gifted the boy with more tongue twisters, more tantalizing tales, until the boy had to cease, intoxicated, bathed in inspirational juice, perfumed in woman scent, overwhelmed in beauty.

Thus were the first languages on these first lands born.

Thus were shaped the words that would map and name the arterial arteries.

For, quite naturally, and without thought, the boy would arise each morning after, fly as a crow, and sing out in tongue after tongue, language after language, a name for all things worth naming, a story for all things worth telling.

These were the original tongues, whispered first by once muted children, who heard the crow, and who then moved their little *tongues, given new sounds, new meanings, so that language graced the new land.*

It was the boy's tongue that sang this to the winds.

It was Bear Woman's juices that allowed it to be.

Charm

"Is it true then," he asks, "that your people strip the skin, eat the flesh and partake of the blood of their enemies? For this I have heard."

Pocahontas unties her cap, takes it off slowly, and shakes the rain from her hair. She looks at the playwright and smiles. She realizes he is in earnest and this amuses her all the more.

"It is a habit we have. It is no big deal. We do it almost daily." She sees Ben Jonson's eyes widen in fascination, and he takes her hand and leads her to the fire that crackles in his study. He sits her in a stool near the flame's glow, stokes the fire with a few prods of iron, then paces the room, hands behind his back. "Is it to distill the spirit of your enemies? Or be it to gain their strength through their consumption?"

"Oh, all that and often just our rapacious appetites," she teases. He strokes his red beard, considering this, as she holds her hands out to the fire, warming them.

"Or you may consider, Sir, that it is little different," she suggests, looking at him, "than your drinking of the blood of Christ or partaking, symbolically perhaps, of the wafer."

He seems perplexed by this, mumbles something, then shrugs and pulls a long pipe from his pocket, and tobacco from its bag, fills the bowl and lights it. He inhales, and sighs softly, contentedly, and offers the pipe to Pocahontas, who shakes her head.

Warmed, she walks the small room, surveying the book-lined walls, the papers strewn everywhere, the quills and inks and scribbling, as Ben Jonson finishes his smoke, all the while studying her intently.

He walks to his desk, opens a drawer, and removes an embroidered satchel.

"I have had this prepared for you. It is a gift and I would be most honoured were you to consent to wear it around your neck. At the least, my lady, if you were to wear it for a single day."

She is torn. Thoughts of her husband so recently lost swirl guiltily in her thoughts along with an odd attraction to this playwright who has befriended her and opened the city to her. She would be at a loss without him, yet her dependence on him bothers her. And the gift feels laden with portent. But she nods.

Ben Jonson walks behind her, as she lifts her hair out of the way, and he delicately places the string under her laced reticella collar and ties it at the back of her neck.

There is a slight, pleasant scent.

"What is it I smell?" Pochahontas asks.

"It is the scent of marigold, dill and lemon balm, my lady. It is what we call a love potion."

She smiles, deciding at the moment she will wear it.

If only for the day.

*"...Tabacco, Nectar, or the Thespian spring,
Are all but LUTHERS beere, to this I sing..."*

– Ben Jonson

Departures

Throngs of hastening sailors and workers line the dock. The rush of footsteps, stacking of provisions and rolling of barrels is at a fevered pace. The ship is due to part with the river's tide and that event of the moon is not to be missed. The Captain stands nervously, eyeing the sun's position and the still formidable stock of wares on land, waiting to be boarded. Ben Jonson stands aside, slightly piss'd, as he has spent the morning in the Rooster's Cock with Inigo Jones, quaffing tankard after tankard. Inigo now stands beside him, also tipsy, lighting his tobacco and watching the hustling bustle of the dockhands.

"Bears! Indians! Beavers! I confess a jealousy of the adventures that await you and an inclination to toss my commitments aside and join you on your voyage," Inigo says.

"Aye. Your company would be most welcome, I suspect. Though in our debates aboard perhaps we will have stabbed each other long before we reach those noble shores."

Inigo laughs, then slaps him on the shoulder.

"Have you imbibed as yet in that noble princess's unseen pleasures?"

Jonson looks to him and laughs.

"No, it is a goal to which I still aspire and it is not for want of trying, but she does protect it more steadfastly than a Papish nun true to the faith in a French convent. Still, I am not a man to be dissuaded from such delights."

"Your dedication to that art I do appreciate. And she truly be a noble savage indeed. Nature's perfection no less, unlike our women, who are spoiled by the billows and debris of having matured in our cities. Perhaps a farm girl comes close to the savage woman, but even there, there is a lack. The reverberations of our cities spread far and spoil the fairest of maids."

"Indeed," Jonson replies. "'Tis our fortune to live in an age where the world has become a village and one has only to travel, as if across the pasture, to a new farm, where untouched wonders await plucking."

"And so you follow her back to the Americas."

"Indeed. In the week since she departed I have thought of little else but her. She is becoming my font, the spark that shall inspire my greatest masque."

"Then," Inigo says, clapping him on the shoulder, "I wish you fair voyage, absent of gale and pyrates and beastly monsters of the deep. Speed thee safe to Virginia's pristine shores."

The young woman takes to the stage in her fringed, buckskin miniskirt, her eagle-feathered headband, and her beaded bra sparkling with jewels. Twenty-one, full breasted, round bottom, wide hips; she shakes her ass on the stage while the high-techno, electro-powwow, traditional drums pound rhythms behind her.

Near the dance stage a table of bored civil servants on extended lunch gaze upon her hopefully; a few bored salesmen are scattered around texting, one or two old-wankers, and a single boisterous table of construction workers who let out a spontaneous cheer.

It promises to be the best dance they've seen this afternoon.

In a far corner, unnoticed in the dark, sits Bear Woman. She is drawing little liquid scribblings on the plastic table with the condensation from her draft glass. Each claw-drawn scribbling a portal, uniting past and present.

On stage she bends, back facing the leering eyes of those near her. The bureaucrats, who are loosening ties, are trying to cover hardening erections with their Blackberries, as she grabs her ankles, her skirt raised and her buckskin G-string the only minute item covering her rounded rear.

As the leather hem rises, a small tattoo is revealed. A little dancing bear on her right buttock. And from the back of the room there is suddenly an enormous, approving bellow that shakes the room, makes lights flicker, causes every head to turn, and brings a smile from the dancer.

Seas

Across the crest of the rising wave, the churning sea blown hard by the northwesterly, he sees the dark ship emerge, yet again.

A moment later, a bright orange and white flash and then the boom of the cannon. A few seconds later the cannonball hits the water's surface, sending a geyser high in the air. Much, much closer this time.

Ben Jonson has never seen a buccaneer but he has seen renderings of Blackbeard in broadsheets back home and this is inspiration enough for him to imagine the lot huddled by the chaser, peering through the mist at their prey. Smoking long matches wrapped in their beards, dreadlocks hanging down under broad-brimmed hats adorned with exotic plumage, and tattooed fingers clutching jeweled daggers taken from dead Moors.

The ship's captain and two Negro sailors stand beside Ben Jonson and they all look grim and nervous, which gives little comfort to their passenger.

"She is getting closer," one of the Negroes observes, and the Captain of the *The Nutmeg* nods silently and casts a glance at the playwright. For a moment Ben Jonson feels he is being appraised, his value measured.

For his part the Captain is thinking just that. Can this obnoxious playwright buy their lives and safe passage? Will his potential ransom save his ship?

At that moment dejection casts a bitter pall over the Captain's face. He is aware of the rules. In the act of being caught by pyrates there is no bargaining to the game. A tear wells in the Captain's eye, knowing a swift dump into the cold, cold Atlantic will be his fate, while the playwright at his side will be a valued prize and kept alive for ransoming.

What justice in this? A lifetime of sea experience and hard work to end as shark feed, while this foppy artiste, who has never mastered an honest trade, is spared and traded for gold.

The Captain's gaze turns back to the black ship in pursuit. No, he cannot permit a capture. It would be an effrontery to common sense.

A cannon shot.

A sudden rip.

A lurch to starboard.

The planks groan as the aftsail crashes to the deck.

The Captain lowers his head and cries as the two Negroes cross themselves.

And Ben Jonson, regardless of whatever trepidations swirl under his skin, smiles, knowing he is about to meet his first true pyrates.

The young woman turns, and bends forward, her long fingers cupping each breast and squeezing them. She winks, and out of her bra pulls a page of parchment. The civil servants are the only table that knowingly gasp, for, as she holds it up to the light, they see it for what it is – a perfect copy – surely not the real thing, though they collectively fantasize it is – of the Royal Proclamation of 1763.

She winks seductively, rolls the parchment into a tube and rubs it up and down her sacred mound.

Years of pent-up reserve evaporates in an instant and the civil servants rise from their chairs, cheering and lewdly whistling, to the surprise of the construction workers and the amusement of the Bear, who claps together two mighty paws in joyous appreciation.

Captive

"He may be worth a pretty penny but then maybe he not be," the distinctly female voice comments.

Ben Jonson turns to see the figure approach, dressed in red jacket, black hat and tan leggings. Her hair is red and long tresses hang down from under a hat adorned with silver and gold trinkets that shine and sparkle in the midday sun's reflection.

But it is her face that stuns Jonson. High cheekbones, flashing green eyes and red lips that at this moment are curled malevolently at the corners as the female sizes up her most recent capture.

"Perhaps he be worth ransoming after all," she says again, pulling a dagger from her waist. "Or not."

She circles the playwright, then lightly presses the blade of her dagger to his throat.

"Perhaps he should join the others?" the portly leader of the pyrates offers, motioning to the waters where the last reminder of the lost crew of *The Nutmeg* can still be seen, a single hat floating on the surface that had belonged to the Captain. Around the playwright, other buccaneers are tearing through crates, rolling barrels down into the hold, and throwing overboard whatever cargo of *The Nutmeg* is of no value in pyrate's currency.

"Calico Jack be my name," the pyrate says, stepping up to Ben and staring him in the eyes. The scent of onion, tobacco and sweat staggers the playwright, who pulls back as the woman behind him titters then takes hold of his head and presses the blade.

"Fish food or ransom?" she asks.

Calico Jack shrugs.

"If he be who he say he is, the King's playwright indeed, perhaps he will fetch us a pocket full of gold. But if he be lying then we have wasted good food and water on him, just to get him to Providence. I leave his fate to you, Annie-dear."

"Well, my friend," she whispers in his ear. "It appears you are mine. Your fate is in my hands. Hmmm, what shall it be?"

Ben Jonson turns his head, very delicately, toward her.

"Oh, I would say 'spare me' would be the wise choice, Madame. For my loss would be a tragedy of epic proportions to the world. Permit me to introduce myself. I am Ben Jonson, Royal Playwright to His Ever Glorious and Generous and Non-forgiving, I might add, Majesty King James. I don't believe I've had the pleasure…"

"Shush you!" She smacks him on the head, hard.

"I am Annie Bonnie, servant to no man or 'Monarch', and I know who you claim to be. You are now my captive nonetheless and regardless. Whether I shall permit you to live aboard this ship, this *Mystical Lady*, we shall see. You must earn your keep, for while this *Lady* is the freest world there is sailing the seven seas, she be very fickle and particular on who she allows to stay. We shall play a little game. See if you are indeed a muse. A little challenge for you I do prescribe."

"A test?" he queries. To which she nods, a grin forming on her most lusciously cruel lips.

"You shall have to sunset, Sir." She ponders the sky momentarily. "That would give you, I believe, two hours to compose me a sonnet, a most magnificent sonnet, or you shall be visiting the sharks, like your former friends.

"A sonnet? A sonnet to what?" Jonson asks.

"Why to my beauty, of course." She laughs, pressing the blade just hard enough to make a little river of blood on the pale Englishman's throat.

"You do agree I am of a nature to inspire the greatest verse. Do you not?"

He nods, feeling the slow trickle flow from his throat.

"A sonnet, then, of beauty such as the English world has never seen."

She saunters away.

"Surely I am inspiration enough." She laughs a last time, over her shoulder, with a toss of her hair.

Bear Woman sits on her haunches at the corner of Bloor and Bay. She is the hot contraire at the corner of haute couture. A humungous, flea-bitten mound of brown fur in a neighbourhood where elegant anorexia is the ultimate aspiration. This bear is not easily ignored. She is living fur amongst the faux fur.

Bear Woman is a rambling, shambling artifact of the past. A misplaced mystic. A lingering echo of forgotten tales. The unconscious utterings of shaman visioning in drunken stupor. This bear growls, snaps at high heels, swipes at glittering bags, and sings the praises of the last true wild Indians, those on the street with their bottles in hand.

Bear Woman pants in the heat, her parched tongue longing to lap from the waters of long paved-over streams. The crowds of bag-wielding shoppers part as they approach her. Most look straight ahead or away from her. She is a reminder of something they can't quite place but that makes them distinctly uneasy.

She pisses, and her yellow stream flows down the sidewalk outside Holt Renfrew and into the sewer grate, replenishing the ancient arteries.

Her invisible host of lice and fleas seeps off her, onto the sidewalk, past doormen, and into the très chic store.

Bear Woman cackles.

Critique

"It is not bad," she says, having read it in a soft whisper to him. "Not bad?" Ben Jonson twitches. This pyrate woman, who knows nothing of art or the fine world of the theatre, let alone a sonnet, the poetry of the King's scribe, nonetheless has the effrontery, the gall, the brashness to pass judgment on a poem, one constructed with her in mind, and then to say, without a smidgen of appreciation, that it is *not bad*.

"Madame," he says the word with a tone that implies the honorific is hardly worthy of her, "this poem is not only a fine example of the seemingly unbounded talents of myself, but may I also remind you it was written under the duress of a threat to my life and with time a factor too. So to call it, as you put it, not bad, is both an insult and a gross misjudgment that does nothing but reveal your, shall I say, lack of knowledge of the poetic arts."

Her eyes flash at him and he sees and feels cold steel and shivers involuntarily, but then she smiles slightly.

"Watch your tongue, boy," she giggles. "'Tis I with the dagger on my hip, and you with your fate in my hands. And, as for your, shall I call them, opinions, let me just say that I find your poetics infused with a certain attractive descriptiveness, but that your flowery interjections are so over-the-top and, well, speak to an age that predates either of us, so that I can't help feeling as if this is German wine, so cloyingly sweet that any depth of substance or taste on the part of the author is lost."

Ben Jonson's jaw drops and he goes to speak, but she quickly puts a forefinger to her lips, quieting him.

"It is, to make my point clear, writing for the court, which in itself is fine. But I do fear your life of indulgences and providing and proffering poetic amusements for the King has made you little more than a jester, albeit of the literary kind."

"What!" he spits out. "Who are you? And…how…where…. You're a woman, a buccanner."

"Shush now." Annie pinches his nose. "I am the daughter of nobility, my father was a Governor of His Majesty's most green and lush island of Jamaica, and I, as you can see, was properly schooled, very properly I might add, and what my tutors failed to teach me, I have learned in my trade. I am skilled in both the delicate arts and the hard-edged currency of the seas. I straddle both." She pauses to smile at him. "And…" she points to the parchment. "This is poetry of a sort. I do not deny that. Does it flatter me? Well, if I was one of your mindless trollops in the court, then yes. But as a *moderne* and educated and independent woman, I can say that this does nothing for me. Not even a smile, let alone a blush, is the effect. Is it enough to save your life? Well, to be frank, no. But perhaps there is a way you can make this up to me, that is, if you are up to the challenge…"

Her hand reaches for his codpiece and squeezes it, rather harshly for Jonson's liking.

"What shall it be? Boy."

Paul Seesequasis

New World Masque

As soon as the King was set, and the Court in its finery in place, in high expectation, with pennants from the trees and the noble savages in attendance, there was heard the sound of trumpets and the strange musick of the tribesmen's Instruments. His Majesty gave his assent and curtains fell back to reveal a stage, bare of all but nature itself, upon which an actor in Bear costume came forth dancing, leading Love, a Native princess bound to the beast by long ribbons of red and white…

Bear leading Love bound…

At which point Ben Jonson leant over and whispered in the Monarch's ear a note of explanation:

"This Bear was understood as brute strength and always the Enemy of Love and Beauty and so lies in wait to entrap innocence. In this case, Antiquity hath given her the upper hand of civilization to conquer, and there find the Face of a Fair Savage Princess: unbound and unspoiled, with no G-d but worship of a land untouched by evil, where she hath the power of the moon's blessed gift to womankind."

Their eyes are drawn to the stage.

BEAR
Come Ladee Love, delicate creature
All the triumphs, all the spoils,
Taken of your lands, and toils,
Over your Father, and over Friend,
O'er your Mother, here it must end.

And, you, now, that thought to lay.
The New World 'tis at waste, 'twas my prey.

LOVE
Cruel Bear, I rather strive,
How to keep my World alive.
And uphold it: close to me,
And protect lest Chaos be.
Tell me Noble Monster, what should move
Thee to spite Love, to disapprove?
Is there nothing honest, nor good,
Nothing bright, or pure in thy blood?
Still, thou art thy self, and perhaps made
Only of greed, and to invade
My chaste bosom. Born of this place,
Will none take pity on my case?
Some soft, soft in you (dare say do I see
A soft spot in thee, that melts for me).
No, but this you can witness bear
Of my candour, when they hear
What thy malice is, or, how
I simply be thy Captive now.
For if I am to fall, innocent I of course be,
And perish with Heaven's Glories hidden with:
In the New World there are
A Sky Woman of the morn,
Ne'er were brighter stars born,
Nor more perfect Beauties seen;
As the children born of this Nature Queen
Of this Turtle Island, and 'twas said,
That she should with the Sky wed.
For which high up and with Grace,
Her Love shone upon all our Race.
Without judgment rendered or concept of sin,
Unbridled and free to dream a world within.

BEAR
Yes, yes but you will find out,
That a world only within is truly a world without.

LOVE
Why? If there be no slaves or servants here,
And Sky Woman give birth to a world fair,
What inspires thy hunger to rule that world?

BEAR
Well, you shall flee in fear.

LOVE
Nay, BEAR, thus far I have stayed near.

BEAR
Yes, but you find out
That World only within is truly a World without.

LOVE
Why? If there be no slaves nor servants here,
And Sky Woman does give birth to a single World fair
What need to be hungry to rule that World?

BEAR
Well, you shall run in fear.

LOVE
Nay, BEAR, thus I have avoided every temptation to flee.

BEAR
Wherein what's done is done, and all I do
Is keep the light, and all wealth and treasure too.

LOVE
That's clear as light to me; for therein lies
That this Lady's power is but in her eyes?
And her body, and soul and grace
And she desires no husband, nor manly wealth, or dower.

BEAR
I spake but of treasure, not of eyes.

LOVE
'Tis beauty we see with our eyes that unites.

BEAR
The eyes deceive whereas money moves, and is fixed.

LOVE
A rolling Eye, that's Native stories in there,
That throws her glances everywhere;
And, being but pure or fair would do
The animals, plants and arts for you.

BEAR
Ah, but the powers and spirits thereof are mixed.
Two Contrary worlds I do see.

LOVE
That's Smiles, and Tears,
And Sun, and Moon; for either bears
or other beasts gives reprieve.

BEAR
As is time, till now,
That Fate decided our worlds to join, or how.
How now LOVE? Do you pray?
Not another word, to say?

Do you find this conquest, so brutal and long?
In hoping for better you have been at a fault, and wrong.

LOVE
BEAR, it is your Pride, to vex
The world you deal with, and perplex
Things must be easy for you: Ignorance,
Things that are for your self-advance,
Of profits and riches and fortunes to make
Riddles, and mystery and the senses you forsake,
Which came gentle from the Muses,
And bear witness to your countless abuses.

BEAR
Nay, Lady your railing will not save you.
I am ravenous and right now must have you.
Come, my fruitful woman, come forth,
Dance for me, in unashamed nakedness, give worth.
Such be the lot of the Captive, or the whore,
And your Sky Woman's triumph doth prove poor...

LOVE dances as BEAR drools.

BEAR
Now I take you up and carry you high
To the Cliff, where I will tear apart my lady fair
Piece-meal, and treat myself to each a part
Of your raw, tender and bleeding heart.

LOVE
Fair audience, have your wishes no power
To help Love at such an hour?
Will you lose me thus? Adieu,
Think, what will become of you,
Who shall praise this land you admire,

Who shall whisper stories by the Fire.
As you listen, soft tales; who bring you
Ancient tongues, in Rimes, to sing you;
Who shall bathe you in virgin streams,
Cleanse your blood, and soothe your dreams.

A Dialogue between the audience and the BEAR.

BEAR
What gentle nature compels us
To honour Love?
The night sky is bright and white Lights
That grace the Nights
Are shot from Heaven's Eyes
And bless clear and bubbling streams
That are fairer than any in the fairest dream,
And the moon that now doth rise.
Then before this land is lost, or swept away,
We seek to witness that Beauty shines, in every way.
It would Nature quite undo,
For losing these, you lost her too.

The Measures and Revels of the masque follow.

The last Masque-Dance of LOVE.

What just Excuse has affronted agèd Time
Her weary limbs now to have eas'd,
And sate LOVE down without crime,
While every thought and well wish was so much pleas'd!
But BEAR so greedy to devour
His own, and all that he sets forth,
In eating every minute of every hour.
Some miracle of the rarest worth
May still be rescued from his Rage,

Paul Seesequasis

So as not to die by Time, or Age.
For LOVE hath a living Name,
And blessing to Heaven, from whence she came.
The concluding chorus.

BEAR
Now, now, Gentle LOVE be free, and Beauty blest
With the sight untouched and long'd to see.
Let us the muses, sages, and tellers go to rest,
For in their wisdom our temperance may happy be.
Then, then, angry BEAR sound, and retract the claws in your feet,
Learn to move in time, and all measures meet:
Thus should the muses, sages, and tellers go to rest
Bowing to the Sun, singing to the West.

Delights

Rapacious. Insatiable. Violent. Lustful. She is all this and more, the playwright thinks, as Annie straddles him again. He is now tired and needs urging, coaxing, and when she manages to slip it in again, it is now for the playwright a vigorous and taxing trial.

Jonson is no longer the instigator. He is the recipient and he is exhausted.

"Madame, I am afraid I am barely able…"

Annie slaps him.

Laughing as she plunders him yet again.

She bends now, her hair falling in his face, and bites his ear, hard.

Preceded by a whisper in his ear.

"Perhaps I shall decide not to trade you in at all, my little bon-bon."

Taken

Rum and ale freely flow. Such open, unabashed debauchery Ben Jonson has never known, not in the wildest nights in any tavern of olde London. He staggers on the deck, grasping the taft rail for balance, stepping over prone pyrates, singing a seaman's ditty to which the words of fornication suddenly seem poetically-inspired.

Point Negril lies westward, a distant black speck, and the playwright knows there lies his freedom. But he is in no rush to be ransomed. He feels an affinity, not only to this newfound buccaneering life, but also to the odd, wilde woman who he sees now, climbing up the rigging, her lengthy locks flowing in the breeze. This Annie, this "wilde cat" as she is oft called by the crew, has him smitten.

A mound of gaudily coloured cotton moves now near his feet, and Ben Jonson bends down and tries to nudge Calico Jack from his drunken slumber but to no avail. The Captain is dead to the world. Through bottle and battle, capture and pillage, Jonson finds himself now a free citizen of this ship, of this *Mystical Lady*, a happily inebriated and satisfied citizen no less. "Sail ahoy! Starboard!" Annie yells, her voice carrying down to a decidedly non-responsive deck. A few pyrates stir. Those still staggering and vertical to the planking look to the direction she points and move to action, but it is far too few to properly unfurl the sails, raise the anchor or man more than a single cannon.

His lady descends the rigging, swearing and swatting prone bodies with the flat of her sword but to no avail as their doom approaches with the speed of the wind to its back. In ten minutes enemy shot rakes the deck, a broadside tearing gaping holes in the hull, bringing the mainmast crashing down and causing Jonson and Annie and all still walking to kiss the planking as cannonballs arc over them.

The Albion is a ferocious beast, a British man-of-war of the new fashion, built of thick American timbers, and, at the most sober of times, the *Mystical Lady* would have hauled to the wind, outsped her, and made good her escape. Today however she is prone and drunk and defenceless to her honour as grappling hooks land and take hold of her and sailors with cutlasses in their teeth and pistols in their sashes swing aboard. "Had you fought like men you would not hang like dogs!" are the last words Ben Jonson hears uttered by Annie as she is led away.

Jonson himself is on his knees, feeling less the pyrate and more the fool.

Bear Woman watches from the edge of the woods, her head resting on her front legs, her ears upright. The humans are busy, the machinery hums, the wrecking ball swings, the sledgehammers tear through concrete. White dust clouds disperse in the breeze, and chunks of rubble are the only remnants of the Beaver Theatre.

Bear Woman remembers the striptease. The sacred dance. The honouring of the earth. She feels an inclination to spring up, roar across the streets, and tear the flesh of the humans before her. But she doesn't.

She simply watches.

Wrecked

Gale winds blow and rains slash across the brig as it flounders, tossed and helpless, near treacherous shoals. Timbers crack, moan and protest, and wave after wave lifts and submerges and toys with the ship while the heavens, black and cloud-laden, save for the crash of thunder and blaze of lightning, roar endlessly.

There is a crack, an enormous surge of water, and upon the crest of the wave the ship is overturned, smashed and scattered, and souls fall into the tumult of the sea, amongst them a playwright, knocked unconscious by a barrel of salted-pork.

AMERICA

"Smoking is a custom loathsome to the eye, hateful to the nose, harmful to the brain, dangerous to the lungs, and in the black, stinking fume thereof nearest resembling the horrible Stygian smoke of the pit that is bottomless."

– James I

Beached

He awakens on a narrow beach, the surf washes over him, broken timbers from the doomed ship float up nearby. The momentum of a wave pushes him forward, and he rides the crest of water over the white sand, towards land. Slowly, he rises to one knee, his hose in tatters, soaked to the bone. Before him towers a mighty forest, darkly imposing in its immensity. The sky is full of birds of every size and shape, wilde and savage species that swoon and dive and cackle endlessly. He has never before seen such feathered creatures. He stumbles forward into the tall grasses that brush his waist, staggers and rolls over the dunes, and then recovers his composure, takes a deep breath, and enters the forest.

What wilde beasts wait within? What sharp fangs now slaver, ready to devour him?

Driven forward by some unexplained pull, he sets forth through branches and trunks and rocks and meadows. On and on as the sun rises, first behind, then above, then finally before him. He sweats and removes his torn doublet and wraps it over his head.

A white-tailed deer looks up at him, quizzically, then deems him no threat and returns to its grazing. The playwright, sans quill or parchment, is left wordless, bewildered by the fragrance of the air, the scent of pine, grass, and flowers sweeter than any perfume devised. He bends down and removes the wet pantofles from his feet, quite ruined, the dye of the slipper having stained his feet a peacock blue. For a moment he stares at his feet, giggling at the colourful digits. Why was he wearing these? He shrugs and tosses them to the wind.

The woods are dense now. The sun breaks through only in infrequent beams of light. Everywhere is beastly chatter, as if he has become the topic of beastly conversation. Birds, strange rodents, scurrying feet, hopping amphibians, move about him and he is quite overwhelmed, flustered, fox witted. Then ahead, a clearing, a colourfully flowered meadow, and he stops at the edge, taking stock, panting and recovering his breath.

Ahead he sees a house. Well, not a house proper but a construction. Reassuringly he tells himself it must have been made by human hands. He walks toward it, cautiously, searchingly, but there is no movement, no attired servant emerges to greet him. He reaches the home, sees it is an abode of hides unknown and branches pulled into a concave shelter. Not Whitehall Palace but a safe abode nonetheless, he mutters to himself, as he lifts the hide flap and kneels, enabling him to crawl inside.

His pupils adjust slowly. At first all is dark, but gradually light prevails and shapes form. A circular interior, and there, opposite, a pile of furs that now take on the familiar shape of a human body. He goes to stand, bumps his head with a thud on a heavy branch, and learns the value of crouching within such structures. Now, on all fours like a bear, he saunters toward the shape and, softly, says "Hullo."

There is no response, and after pausing for what seems eternity, he pulls the furs aside.

A head, distinctly dark-haired and facing away, a bare shoulder, the gentle curve of a female back, the buttocks, the thighs, down to the ankles, and he stops. Fear is replaced by rapture. He senses the warmth of a woman, more welcoming than any other warmth in G-d's creation. He traces a finger along the slope of her waist, the rise of her hips, the soft decline of her thighs.

She turns to face him. The corners of her lips seductively turn upward. She is unashamed in her nakedness. One nipple lightly touches his calloused hand.

For once he is speechless, in fact sweating, and sensing his rising discomfort, she lifts a finger and places it gently to his lips.

"Sssssh," Pocahontas whispers. "You are home now."

Meadowes

Ben Jonson sits cross-legged and naked in the afternoon sun. He chuckles at his daring, his new found nativeness. He lies on the grass, butterflies and bees circling around him. He runs his fingers over his body, feeling the sweat that has sprung in the warmth of the afternoon sun. He runs his fingers through his still-damp hair. He brings his fingers to his nostrils and inhales. Wondrous, human scent mingled with the faint saltiness of the sea. Now he laughs out loud. No hosiery, britches or expensive perfumery to mask his being. He is truly free now and, closing his eyes, he throws his head back, eyes squinting, and dares the sun to match his stare. As beads of sweat break on his forehead, he falls back, lying arms stretched like Christ in repose. He opens his eyes and watches the clouds skirt across the blue sky, each shaping itself into a costume, an actor on the stage.

Ben Jonson is in love.

It is unheard of. Impossible. Absurd. Would shock the court in London if he were, in fact, in London and not somewhere, who knows where, amidst the American wilderness.

"I shall compose her a masque," he yells, leaping to his feet. "The greatest masque ever conceived under G-d's heaven."

He runs into the meadow, randomly in circles, pausing as if listening for an approaching beast, then skipping, jumping, hopping on one foot. He waves one arm, then the other, points at nothing, and mouths nonsensical words.

Butterflies scatter, blue and yellow flowers bend in the wind, bees hover around him as he does his strange dance, all his limbs and little bits swinging and swaying.

"I proclaim this masque to be in celebration of the meeting of two worlds." He stands still now, chest puffed, as if facing the Royal gala audience. "It shall glow with lights, levity and wisdom. No costumes save the masks. Each actor in resplendent native dress. The masks shall represent the wilde and noble beasts of this fantastic land."

He pulls at his beard in momentary contemplation.

Eureka.

He turns around and around, arms outstretched.

"I shall present it here. In this meadow. I will entreat His Majesty to assemble the greatest fleet England can summon. A mighty host of vessels – not for war, exploration or commerce – but to bring to this meadow the entire court of London, every gentleman and gentlelady with an inclination to appreciate the arts of life.

"For here they shall witness the greatest masque of all time.

"Here!" he yells.

"Here!" facing the other direction.

"Here!" shouting toward the heavens.

"And, at the crescendo, she shall appear. The true, everlasting triumph of beauty. This masque shall be celebrated through time as *Sun's Darling: The glory that is Pocahontas*.

"My greatest creation! My superb inspiration!" he yells over and over until he collapses, sated, on the soft bed of grass.

Tattoo

"What is this?" Pocahontas asks, as she holds Ben Jonson's thumb with her fingers, noticing the tattooed 'T' on the underside of his thumb.

"It is my brand," Jonson says. His other hand caresses her, trying to slip the dress off her shoulder. She stops him and, smiling, shakes her head, not now.

"A tattoo signifying what?" Pocahontas asks, knowing that all brands, no matter how seemingly insignificant, contain a story. Jonson sighs at the gentle rebuff, realizing his efforts to consummate his liaison with his princess of the Americas are to be thwarted a bit longer, and leans back on the furs. She sits cross-legged, facing him, dark eyes flashing expectantly for the story.

"'Twas almost 20 years ago. A young man's passion, the foolishness and vanity of youthful pride," he begins.

"A fellow actor, Gabriel Spenser, I see his handsome face still in my dreams, insulted my pen to friends. Said I was no more than a poor man's Shakespeare, a toady to the great man. I demanded he retract, to which he refused, despite every opportunity I afforded him, and I had no recourse."

Jonson shrugs. Pocahontas nods.

"So we met, one crisp fall morning, in the meadows outside London. Him, I and a host of actors and followers of the stage. He had his rapier and I had forgotten mine, so I borrowed from a friend. Unfortunately, his dagger was a full 10 inches shorter when we drew blades. I recall his grin, as if he expected me to forfeit, which I most assuredly did not. I demanded we continue.

"Well, when steel met steel it was soon apparent his swordsmanship was of the stage variety only, that when life was on the line, and real blood was in question, he had no heart for it. Despite his advantage of size, every parry, every lunge was mine and I pondered giving mercy, but darker demons took hold, and I ran him through, twice, to the stomach. His death was slow, and as they attended to him, and I wiped his blood from my blade, I felt a contentment I cannot describe."

"So the 'T' is a tattoo of victory?" Pocahontas inquires.

"A warrior's mark?"

"No," Jonson replies, shaking his head.

"It is a mark of shame. The 'T' is for Tyburn, the gallows to which I was condemned to hang. Being a commoner, my fate was to feed the ravens. And so it would have been except for the Bible."

"The Bible? G-d saved you?" She smiles, leaning forward, enraptured.

"In G-d's way. Yes," Jonson confesses. "You see, as an actor I am little more than a pauper. Even worse, I am considered a rogue, a creature of ill repute, as, by necessity, are so many who chose to flout, shall we say, the scriptures. So death be my fate except for a little clause known as the "Benefit of the Clergy" which states that an educated man, no matter how low in standing, may escape the hangman's noose once, if he is able to quote a passage from the Bible in Latin."

"And you did, happily for us," she smiles.

"Yes, at the cost of all my worldly possessions, which, being a struggling actor in those days, was no great loss."

Pocahontas laughs.

"And what passage did you quote?"

"Ecclesiastes 1:9." He reverts to Latin: "Nothing under the sun is new, neither is any man able to say: Behold this is new: for it hath already gone before in the ages that were before us."

"Wise words," Pocahontas remarks. "You hold these to be true to this day?"

He looks at her, studies her intently for a moment, and shakes his head.

"Upon meeting you, no longer. I look at you and the sun is new. The land is wondrous and wilde. Untouched. Virginal. Speaking of which."

His hand slips under her dress, up her soft thigh.

She stops him with her hand.

"It is not time…yet."

She looks up at the full moon and smiles.

She is away from the pack and tonight will hunt as she prefers.

Alone.

Between the seams of colonial boundaries she roams.

Silent. Predatory. Hungry. Seductive weetigo. Enchanting princess. She hides behind trees where she watches and waits. She is patient in her desire; insatiable and endless. A constant arousal, a wetness that drips from her folds onto the forest floor, is sponging the ground where she stands.

Her voice comes from deep within. From her lungs it rises.

Primal. Seductive. When he comes down the path, unsuspecting, she moans softly, causing him to pause. Hearing her he sighs. She emerges and he can only stare, wide-eyed, at her beauty. She sighs and sighs again as he lowers his weapon, slips his armor off, until he is as naked as she. She sways around him, a slow hypnotic motion, as she blows softly, her breath warm on his skin.

Lost

He has gone too far. Too far. He stops, takes a deep breath, vainly seeks his bearings. Every tree is new, every rock and bush a discovery. He swears he has retraced his steps a dozen times, but now, he realizes, obviously to no avail.

Wiping his brow, Ben Jonson sits on a rock and contemplates his plight. Clearly, the buckskin leggings, loincloth, deer jacket and moccasins that she has given him, and in which he is now attired, have done little to make him a man of the forest. Worse, they have inspired a false confidence that has wrought his present folly.

He is no Indian, he says to himself. No Indian at all. No, he is a fool, a clown, a buffoon, an idiot lost in paradise.

He feels the knife sheathed and strapped to his thigh but it is small comfort. Yes, he has stabbed and killed a man, an actor, but he has no clue about how to catch and kill an animal, let alone eat it. Then a more discomforting thought. What protection be this knife against the wildeer, larger beasts that may be eyeing and sizing him up at this very moment? He shudders.

Ben Jonson feels fear. The fear born of his realized insignificance in this vast wilderness; the sudden dawning that he is a mere speck, a piece of fluff at the mercy of the merest whim of nature, a target in the food chain, a woefully weak slab of flesh and bone, barely able to walk on two legs. He is worse than a newly born fawn which is at least blessed with an innate sense of survival.

"Pocahontas!" he yells.

A brief break in the buzzing sounds of the forest but nothing more.

"Pocahontas!" he screams in the other direction, cupping his hands around his mouth to carry the voice.

Time passes, how long he can only speculate. What use now are his masques? His plays? His scribbling? How frivolous and distant now is the Royal Court, the courtesans, fops, every whore and sycophant that had nourished his own sense of self-importance.

The cracking of a dry branch is the only warning, and suddenly the weight of a body knocks him to the ground and he is on his back, winded and looking up at two dark eyes circled in red ochre, a brown face, a long nose with a bone insert, and a broad grin. Ben Jonson feels the knife at his throat, pressing with enough weight to break his skin, a trickle of red blood emerging like a misplaced smile, the smell of leather, sweat, tobacco filling his senses – and the thought flashes through his mind that if he is to die, then there can be no better demise than at the hands of this strong, savage warrior who now leers down at him, sitting on his chest.

For his part the warrior is amused at the oddity of his catch. This stringy, red-haired, bearded European in Indian dress. For a moment the warrior contemplates completing the kill, slitting the throat so that the stream of blood will gush and gurgle, and then to take the blade and slice that rare red hair from his scalp, for on his belt that adornment will surely pack some medicine. But he doesn't.

Rather, he reaches back, pulls the tomahawk from his deerskin belt, and whacks Ben Jonson on the temple with a resounding thud.

She calls forth the sounds of the forest. Her fingertips, like tree branches, entangle him in her roots. Her legs, like tree trunks, wrap around, squeezing him tight. Her mouth, so close now. The lips like the deepest red of a stag's blood, near his, almost touching. She stretches, runs her leaves over him, watching him rise, hard and dripping. Seeking gratification he pleads.

Too late. She spins branches around him. On the cusp of ejaculation he is enraptured, bound, encased in layers of bark that wrap like serpents on to the other. His face is the last shape to disappear, until it too is nothing more than a bump on a tree. The ferocious walker giggles at her mischievousness, then she skips back into the seams of the forest. The dark space that marks the boundary to the wild. The rustle of branches in the wind. The whisper of leaves in the dark. She exhales and awaits the next moon.

Gone Native

A woman's caring touch is unmistakable, even in a dream state, and Ben assumes he is in such a state, feeling the feminine fingers running down his face. But the opening of an eye brings a blurred vision, a kaleidoscope of colours spilling upon him, and a female face but inches away, the brush of her hair on his chin and throat: which, as his focus improves, reveals itself to be long tresses as blonde as the sun. No Indian this, but a woman distinctly civilized, yet attired, as his gaze drifts down to her bosom, in the manner of a savage.

Such a puzzle.

In seconds, images open in his mind: a warrior's face, the smell of man sweat, the striking of polished stone to skull plate; and with that, a throbbing reality floods his senses and he moans in sudden acute pain.

"Sssssh," the female whispers. "It will pass. You have a lump on your skull the size of a potato but you may yet survive. The fever has broke."

With that, he notices her other hand is caked in oozing mud which he sees she is delicately patting on the side of his head from which the most striking pain seems to be coming. He gasps with each soft touch, for no matter how light the touch, the pain is well nigh unbearable.

He is lying on some raised platform in some great hall. Long. One room. Not constructed of marble or brick but of logs. He sees smoke drift toward an open sky in a raised roof which is also the source of light that shines in through the haze. He hears the murmur of many voices, in a tongue he does not recognize. In the distance, he senses there are many in this long house. The sound of adult voices, of children playing, of dogs barking.

Each poultice, herb, incense that she administers and every song she sings brings the playwright further back from the brink. The bulb on his head, originally the size and almost approximate color of a turnip, slowly subsides, the fevers become less frequent, and the delusional dreams dissipate. It is tireless commitment, and Falbo sits by his side, feeling satisfaction as the grip of death lessens and life's vibrancy returns.

For his part Jonson feels himself stepping back from death's door, and his consciousness arises from the murk of doom toward light, till he opens his eyes one morn, as the scent of burning wood fills his nostrils, and looks up and sees her.

"Welcome back."

He nods. Her face takes shape.

"I am Falbo," she says. "You have been put in my care."

"I am a prisoner?"

She nods. "A captive, yes, but not a corpse. Be grateful for G-d's blessing on that. Had they wanted you dead you would not be here."

"Where am I?" Jonson asks.

"A longhouse. You are a captive of the Kanien'kehá:ka, or the Iroquois, as you may know them."

"What shall be my fate?"

She shrugs, applies a poultice. Gently.

"You are English?"

Falbo nods. "I was."

"Was?"

"Was."

"Meaning."

"No longer."

She tells him of her captivity. How her cabin was attacked one fall day by a group of warriors. Her husband, brother, mother and two sons killed. She had been spared, trussed up and taken through trails and woods to here. And, how at first her treatment had been rough, but then, over time, she had been given more liberties. The clan mothers had taught her skills, a warrior had taken her as his, and now she was, well, human.

He studies her.

Then he drifts away in sleep.

She lies on her back.

The cub is coming now.

Her water has broken, the puddle forms beneath her buttocks.

She grabs a fallen branch and bites hard on it with each recurring contraction, each burning wave that courses through her body.

The pack is silent, keeping distance, pacing, nervous, on edge. Only the lead male is still and in sight. He watches as she pushes and sweats and grimaces.

Finally the head, the shoulders and the rest emerge, as the cub slides out in a liquid glide to the earth between her thighs. With effort, she rises slightly to pick the cub up and place it, all wet and slippery, on her belly. She watches as the cub makes its way to her breast.

It finds the nipple, bites so she winces, then starts to suck.

She closes her eyes only a moment, lets strength rise, then reaches with her fingers for the placenta pooling beneath her, and lets its stickiness coat her fingers.

She brings each finger to her mouth and sucks it.

Escape

Birds awaken him. The strangest, oddest twirping and chittering. One moment pleasant, seductive, and the next piercing and painful. A mocking caw, a loving song.

It is the second morning since Ben Jonson's escape and he feels astounded that he is still free, if being on the run and lost in the immensity of the forest can be truly called freedom. He looks at his ankle. It is purple and swollen and most tender to the touch. It singes like hot embers when he puts weight on it. Lifting himself gingerly and, with his newfound walking stick in one hand and using the tree for support with the other, he is able, slowly, to raise himself.

He listens, above the chorus of birds and other creatures, for the sound of crackling branches, the faint echo of human voices, but there is nothing.

Perhaps they have given up.

Maybe he is truly free.

For a moment Ben Jonson feels guilt. It is a strange and odd sentiment for him and, for a moment, he cannot place it. He ponders whether Falbo will be blamed and punished for his escape. He was, after all, in her charge. Indeed, she had pleaded to her sceptical warrior that she could be trusted to keep him in tow, and Ben Jonson had, to her face, assured her he would try no escape.

No, she is to blame for her fate, he decides, for the foolishness of believing in him.

The look in her eyes when he had pushed her down. Such hurt. Such a pained look as he reached for her waist, retrieved the knife, and cut the binding rope free. It was a minute before she uttered anything, called the warrior back. Just enough time for him to smile at her and then throw himself, rolling, down the precipice.

He knew that look in a woman.

G-d knows he had seen it enough in London.

The poor girl had come to the realization that, in a choice between loyalty to a friend or loyalty to himself, he would always come out ahead.

Whatever her ensuing fate at the hands of an outraged warrior, it was of little consequence. He was free.

He wonders if she curses him as she bears the savage punishments from the warrior.

Well, he has faced curses before.

Nonetheless, he feels a certain regret. Falbo was rather beautiful. A pity she will never get to strut in fancy linen and stockings. He would have liked to see her in that. No, he decides, he will make amends by designing a part for her in his masque.

She shall be an angel. An angel in most ephemeral clothing. He would, with a dip of his quill and a flourish on parchment, grant her immortality. Surely, such a gift of his would negate any transgression a mortal is capable of committing under G-d's Heaven.

Soul at ease, Ben Jonson puts his walking stick forward and resumes his trek.

Blackness. Blood red blackness. Nothing else.

Dead?

No.

Ben Jonson sees himself in the royal dais. Pipe in hand.

The sweet taste of tobacco.

Am I the king? He chuckles. He feels wetness, puts his hand to his temple, looks at his hand, and sees blood.

He brings his fingers to his lips. It is red, sticky and tastes like fine wine. Well, fancy that, he thinks.

He looks to the stage and sees Pocahontas. She is resplendent in a white buckskin gown beaded black, a mask to her face, adorned with multi-coloured feathers and jewels. She looks toward him, holds wilde strawberries in her outstretched palm, as if in offering to him, and smiles.

He aches for her.

From the shadows of the stage the warrior emerges. Naked and magnificent. He circles Pocahontas. He has no mask, no adornments. He peers up toward the dais, sees the author, and grins.
Ben Jonson slinks back in his chair, trying to avoid the penetrating eyes, the masculine power so absent in the playwright, now directed toward him. He hides his face in his hands.

The theatre spins.

There is a bear beside him.

A huge bear.

A rather stinky bear.

It stares at him with beady eyes.

He feels small.

Small enough to be a tasty morsel.

The bear smiles.

The playwright had not realized bears could smile.

And then blackness.

Found

Mosquitoes and black flies. It is all he knows and the swelling is now swelling upon the swelling and he has long since surrendered to the insects, ceased to swat or swipe or cover. The playwright barely stumbles forward and now the lightest branch is an obstacle insurmountable till finally he stops and crouches and cries and decides it is here, in this G-d forsaken swamp, that he will die.

The pristine forest has turned on him. Every tree, every bush, ominous and angry, is closing in on him, and the sun is hidden somewhere above, its light scarcely a comfort. Day is night and night is day, and the playwright surmises it is here that his brilliance will be extinguished and his flesh consumed by wilde beasts and his bones spread by scavenging crows and coyotes, when he hears voices and the sound of people approaching. Ben Jonson calls out, in a croaked voice. Should it be hostile savages, he is prepared to die and see to it that his misery may not be prolonged.

The voices stop and then he sees the warrior's party approaching. He falls to his knees, preparing for his end, a whack to the head he assumes, with a blunt tomahawk, when to his wonderment, they study but do not strike him. And then water is put to his parched lips and a blanket wrapped around him, and then he is gently picked up on the back of a strong savage and carried to his salvation.

Bear Woman digs. Beneath the concrete and steel. Under pipes, plastic bottles, Tim Hortons cups, discarded diapers, Big Mac styrofoam containers, clawing and clawing through sewer pipes, fibre-optic cables and long-forgotten stone foundations.

Bear Woman is unlayering the city. Burrowing through time.

Finally, her claws, worn and bloody, break through. She swipes away the final vestiges of man and reaches the stream.

It flows clear, over stones, amongst green foliage and sunlight. Resplendent with frogs, minnows and water bugs. She lowers her muzzle and laps with her parched tongue. Each drop of water is good.

Her round ears perk up and she takes stock, listening to the gurgle of the stream over the stones, soothed by the endless birdsong.

Bear Woman has dug deeper than the girl and the wolves.

She has dug deeper than the boy.

It is just her now.

A bear.

And the stream.

Her stream.

Her first.

She claws a den, near the edge of the embankment and lays herself down and snoozes.

Her dreams are, for once, just light, and she feels, again, what it is to be a bear.

Royal Decree

King James I holds the gold, royally scribed, sealed and embossed quill in his slender fingers and pauses, staring for a moment at the tapestry hanging on the wall, a lion on its hind legs, biting into the throat of a unicorn in its death throes, and sees not the death scene but something beyond it, and hesitates.

Posterity is his obsession, so much so that his closest ministers subtly scold him, implore him to think in the present and not guess the future, or more precisely, how the future will judge him. He had considered his Bible his crowning achievement; that in the act of bringing together the wisest council of men to interpret and dare to rewrite in G-d's name, that the royal legacy was ensured in perpetuity.

And so had his inner court agreed.

But now, if he was to believe his ministers, he was on the verge of eradicating all that he had achieved. To a man, an unprecedented consensus had been reached that His Highness risked blemishing his legacy by embarking on an enterprise that would be sheer folly.

More so, his closet ministers chided, there was rising corruption, depleted coffers and disgruntlement among the nobility to address. Surely, the summoning and dispatching of a great fleet to the Americas in order to put on a masque was, and they said this cautiously, knowing his temper, perhaps best, albeit reluctantly, left to a better time when the Kingdom was overflowing with Cornucopia's fruits and wines.

James sighs.

Closes his eyes.

No.

It is insanity.

It will not do.

Therefore it must be.

He presses point to parchment and ink flows.

"...The many pleasures that I bring. Are all of youth, of heat, of life, of spring..."

– *Ben Jonson*

"Grrrrrrrrrrrrrrrrrrrrrrrrrrrrrrrr..."

– *Bear Woman*

Consummation

It is in the manner in which the petticoat slips from Pocahontas's shoulder that it begins. The silk slips to reveal her small left breast, and his eyes settle upon it and the nipple as she speaks to him of the masque. Ben Jonson lifts a finger to touch her nipple, and this time she takes a breath, looks him in the eyes, but does not stop him.

And, as wig and breeches, petticoat and linen drawers lie discarded on the floor, the light from a moon full over Jamestown on this clear night bathes the room, and the couple, in its softest white glow.

The buzz of cicadas the only sound apart from their breathing.

EPILOGUE

New Worlds

The world has changed. Once the sea had frightened her with its immensity, but now it makes her feel heroic, predestined. No wave or drenching wind can snatch her soul away. She is on her own mission now. Her vision quest is real. It is not the stuff of dreams.

She clutches the tobacco pouch at her hip and for a moment longs for the bitter taste.

She smiles.

Let the sea and wind carry her.

She opens the pouch and tosses a few crumbs of the dried leaves to the wind.

It was not that she hadn't known water, growing up as a child; indeed her skills with a paddle were renowned in her family, and shamed many of her brothers. And she had swum in rivers and creeks and lakes, and even once at the edge of the big water, but never had she considered crossing it. The idea had seemed ridiculous to a young girl, though she had stood once or twice on the bluffs as a child and pondered what lay on the other side.

If indeed there were another side.

Rumours of the strangers had circulated for years and there was little surprise when the rumours became fact and the

Englanders reached her people. Their strange habits, language, dress and smell had intrigued her.

What has happened after that is all but a dream, an illuminated vision quest, a fable in which two worlds collide.

Pocahontas has left the playwright back in Jamestown, assuring him she will return one day. But she has chosen not to tell the playwright that is unlikely, nor tell him of the life growing inside her. A life planted of his seed. At her encouragement and insistence, though, Jonson has become a prime investor in the Orinonco Tobacco enterprise, but in truth, she is the owner, albeit in secret.

And now she is returning across the big waters, not on her own but with a fleet of protective frigates in tow and cargoes laden with *her* tobacco and, most dear to her, the cargo stirring in her belly.

It has been a choppy and stormy two weeks, and most of the court, returning to London after the masque, are pitching their guts into the Atlantic or lying below in bunks, moaning and crying.

But not she.

She is on the deck, head strong into the breeze.

She is returning to London with a new life and a world to explore and share with her girl.

Pocahontas knows, without a doubt, it is a girl.

A girl born on the cusp of a new, glorious age.

A girl born with the blood of two worlds in her.

She stands on the bow, face drenched by the waves, peering toward the white cliffs that must appear someday.

The heartiest of sailors are taken by her fortitude, her seaworthiness, to the extent they dub her 'Red Persephone'.

Pocahontas simply laughs, rubs her protruded belly and peers eastward, toward the eastern horizon and the faint trace of distant shores.

The young woman carries the wolf cub up the hill. It is hot and humid and a million black flies buzz angrily around her but she is oblivious to their bites. The cub mews and she stops, sits, uncovers her breast and guides a nipple into the baby's tiny mouth.

The cub sucks greedily of her milk.

She hears branches crack and looks up. At the edge of the clearing Bear Woman appears, sniffs the air and then snorts approvingly. Pawing the ground, Bear Woman bellows for the young woman to come.

The young woman pulls the wolf from her breast and, holding it in her arms, walks toward her.

Bear Woman snorts approvingly.

And, though bears don't, smiles.

Fin

Acknowledgements

I am indebted firstly to the many family elders of my youth, most of whom are no longer here, who instilled a love of story, animals and land, and if I have gone to places they would not consider proper, I assume that responsibility with humility.

For my children, Suri and Coltrane, who never cease to amaze and show the patience of the Gods with their oft absent father.

To The Conseil des arts et des letters du Quebec, who years ago gave a grant that first bought the time to imagine – a priceless gift to any writer – merci beaucoup.

To The Banff Centre and a precious week at the idyllic Leighton Studios – such a gift.

Tomson Highway, Denise Bolduc, Sandra Laronde, and many others, for the lasting friendship and also Mary Anne Barkhouse for her art – the wolves and yes the 'Beaver Theatre.' I will visit Mary Anne, when the snakes sleep.

Peter Matthiessen for the inspiration; if one is to have heroes then one should be select.

I am especially grateful to Beatriz Hausner and the publishers of Quattro Books, for their belief in this book, their meticulous attention to it, and for their amazing dedication.

Lastly, Adeena Karasick, who first saw the bears and knows them more intimately than I can ever imagine.